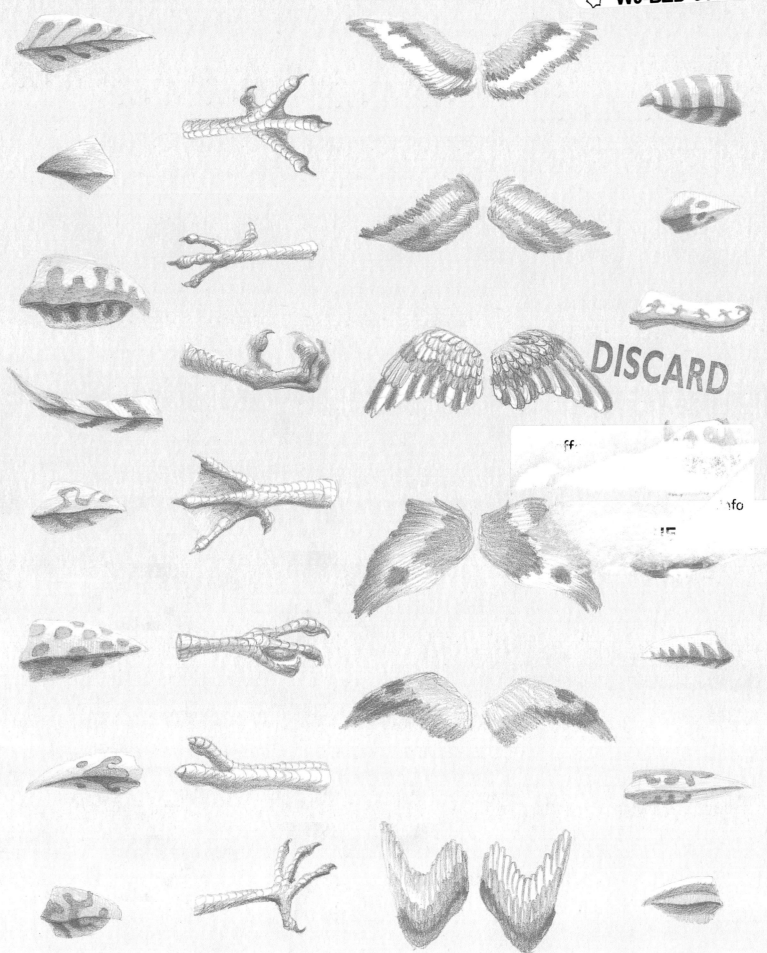

Aviary Wonders Inc.

SPRING CATALOG AND INSTRUCTION MANUAL

Renewing the World's Bird Supply Since 2031

K A T E   S A M W O R T H

Clarion Books ✳ Houghton Mifflin Harcourt ✳ Boston New York

For Maria, Bridget,
John & Evan

Special thanks to David Wiesner. Thanks also to my editor,
Marcia Leonard; my agents, Nancy Gallt and Marietta Zacker; and my husband, Chris Weybright.

Clarion Books • 215 Park Avenue South, New York, New York 10003
Copyright © 2014 by Kate Samworth • All rights reserved.
For information about permission to reproduce selections from this book, write to Permissions,
Houghton Mifflin Harcourt Publishing Company, 215 Park Avenue South, New York, New York 10003.
Clarion Books is an imprint of Houghton Mifflin Harcourt Publishing Company. • www.hmhbooks.com
The illustrations were executed in oil, ink, graphite, and colored pencil. • The text was set in Steam.
Book design by Kerry Martin • Library of Congress Cataloging-in-Publication Data
Samworth, Kate, author, illustrator. • Aviary Wonders Inc. Spring Catalog and Instruction Manual:
renewing the world's bird supply since 2031 / by Kate Samworth. • pages cm • Summary: In a future when deforestation and
other environmental factors have caused many bird species to go extinct, businessman Alfred Wallis offers a catalog of parts for creating
replacements, from hand-carved beaks to Italian-leather feet. • ISBN 978-0-547-97899-4 (hardcover)
[1. Birds—Fiction. 2. Automata—Fiction. 3. Mechanical toys—Fiction. 4. Environmental degradation—Fiction.
5. Catalogs—Fiction.] I. Title. • PZ7.S19453Avi 2014 • [Fic]—dc23 • 2013020247
Manufactured in China
SCP 10 9 8 7 6 5 4 3 2 1
4500448326

All the birds named in "The Right Parts" are real—or once were. The moa, Carolina parakeet,
Javanese lapwing, laughing owl, great auk, caracara, and Haast's eagle are now officially extinct.

ABOUT THE COMPANY

I was born and raised in Lakemont, New York, and discovered a passion for bird watching while working for my family's logging company, first in the Northeast and then in Brazil. I noticed that as the birds' habitat disappeared, their numbers and species declined. As soon as I inherited the company, I shut down operations and devoted myself full-time to building birds. I traveled the world to assemble a team of the finest biologists, engineers, and artisans. Together, we spent two decades on research and development, and in 2031 we put our first bird on the market. We've been selling birds as fast as we can make them ever since.

Aviary Wonders closely copies the form and function of each bird part as it is found in nature and enhances it with patterns and color combinations of our own creation. Everything we manufacture, down to the smallest feather, meets our rigorous standards of beauty and durability. The results are stunning, if I do say so myself, and our birds are built to last.

I know we can't replace the birds that have been lost. But we can provide you with the opportunity to create an exquisite alternative: your very own bird, a work of art you'll treasure for a lifetime.

Alfred Wallis
Founder, Aviary Wonders Inc.

BIRDS TODAY FACE MANY DANGERS:

INSECTICIDES

Habitat Loss

Exotic Pet Trade

CATS!

Some species are disappearing. Others are already gone. Not to worry!

AVIARY WONDERS INC.

· has the solution. ·

Whether you are looking for a companion, want to make something beautiful, or just want to listen to birdsong, we'll supply everything you need to build your own bird. Choose from our catalog of high-quality parts to create the bird that lives in your memory or imagination. Each bird is unique and yours to keep or set free. Imagine the thrill of populating the woods with colorful birds and listening to them sing your favorite songs. That's right! You can even teach your bird to sing. All of our parts are handcrafted and made to order by world-class artisans. And our assembly instructions are simple to follow. Building your own bird is as easy as building a bookcase . . . and twice the fun!

To build a bird the proper way, you'll need more than

·········· You'll also need ··········

the RIGHT PARTS

100% INDIAN SILK
FEATHERS
don't fray with age
like natural feathers

Color Palettes

Old Master:
The reds, golds,
and greens of fall

Tonalist:
Subdued and aquatic
with flecks of sunlight

Impressionist:
The vibrant colors of spring

Minimalist:
Red, white, black,
and bold

BEAKS
CARVED, ENGRAVED,
AND
PAINTED by HAND
in TURKEY

LEGS and FEET
COVERED IN
HAND·TOOLED
Italian Leather

ALL
MOVABLE
PARTS
ENGINEERED
by SWISS
CLOCK-
MAKERS

BODIES

Picture a tiny flightless bird hopping across the keys of your piano or a perching bird large enough to intimidate a housecat. A change of scale transforms the everyday into the fantastic. Your ideal bird is available in any size between 3 inches and 3 feet.

NEW!
Our flightless model for stay-at-home birds

The Moa was large, flightless—and tasty! The last of the species was eaten in the fifteenth century.

SWIMMERS

Duck   Screamer   Guillemot   Swan

Perchers

Bellbird

Bald Crow

Bowerbird

Loved by hat makers, loathed by farmers, the **Carolina Parakeet** was hunted to extinction by 1918.

birds of prey

Vulture

Condor

Kite

Waders

Javanese Lapwing
Last seen in the 1940s

Egret

Heron

Plover

BEAKS

Available in hardwood or porcelain. Spring-loaded hinges allow your bird to feed itself. Choose beak according to diet.

CARNIVORES

For birds of prey

insectivores

For perchers, swimmers, and waders

herbivores

Best for perchers

Curtains for the **Laughing Owl** came around 1914, a few decades after settlers arrived in New Zealand with their cats.

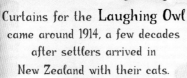

TEACH YOUR BIRD TO CACKLE AND WHOOP IN THIS COLORFUL BEAK.

Warbler

Sparrow

Bushtit

Too beautiful for its own good! Many species of **Macaw** have been driven to extinction by the demands of the exotic pet trade.

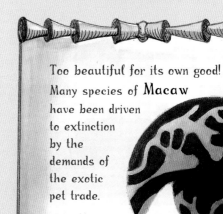

Sora

King Vulture

Tawny Eagle

Cardinal

Crossbill

Dress up your bird for special occasions: 25% off 2nd beak.

PISCIVORES

For waders and swimmers

Avocet

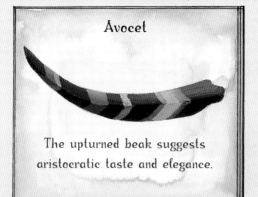

The upturned beak suggests aristocratic taste and elegance.

Pelican

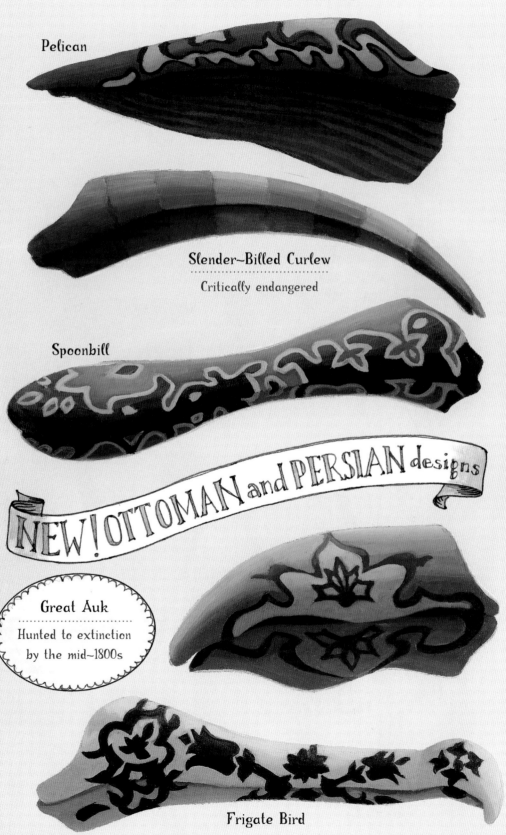

Slender–Billed Curlew

Critically endangered

Spoonbill

Merganser

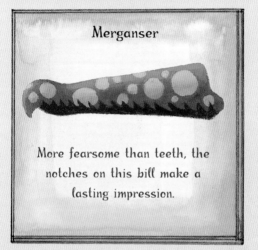

More fearsome than teeth, the notches on this bill make a lasting impression.

NEW! OTTOMAN and PERSIAN designs

Great Auk

Hunted to extinction by the mid–1800s

Hornbill

Part beak, part helmet, and all the romance of a medieval knight

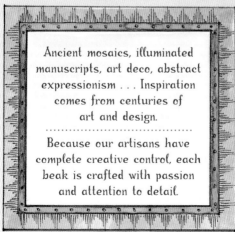

Ancient mosaics, illuminated manuscripts, art deco, abstract expressionism . . . Inspiration comes from centuries of art and design.

Because our artisans have complete creative control, each beak is crafted with passion and attention to detail.

Frigate Bird

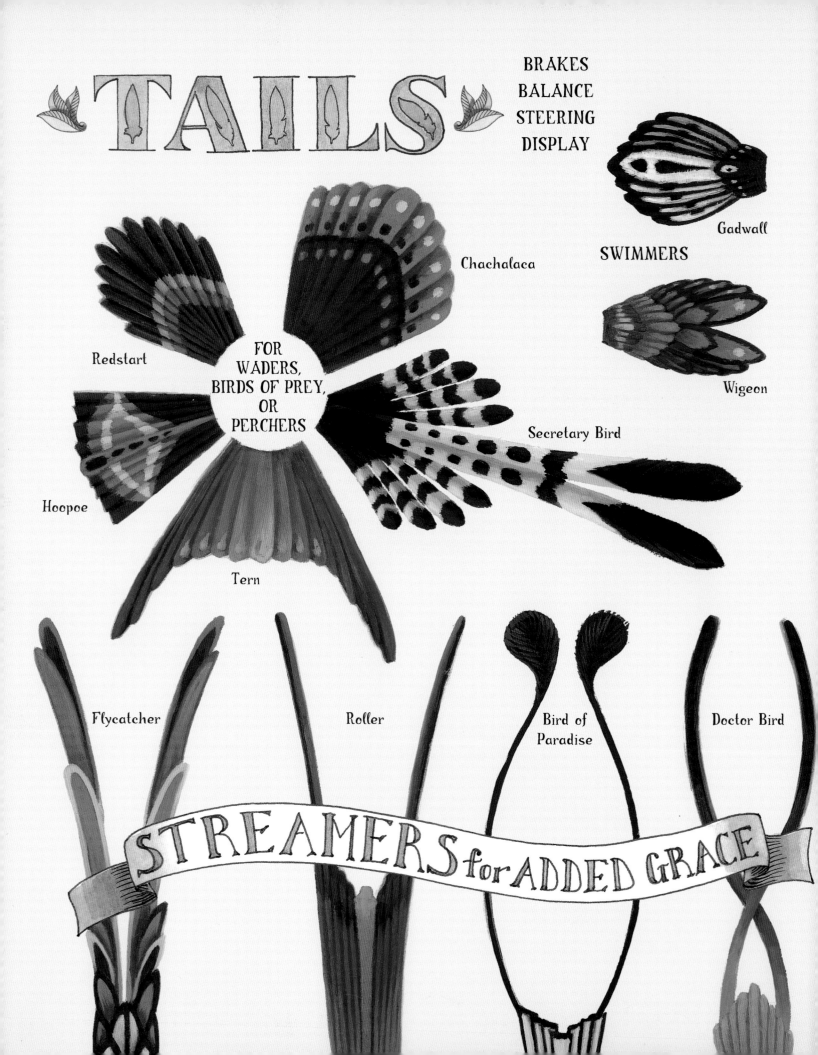

TAILS

BRAKES
BALANCE
STEERING
DISPLAY

Gadwall

SWIMMERS

Chachalaca

Redstart

FOR
WADERS,
BIRDS OF PREY,
OR
PERCHERS

Wigeon

Secretary Bird

Hoopoe

Tern

Flycatcher

Roller

Bird of
Paradise

Doctor Bird

STREAMERS for ADDED GRACE

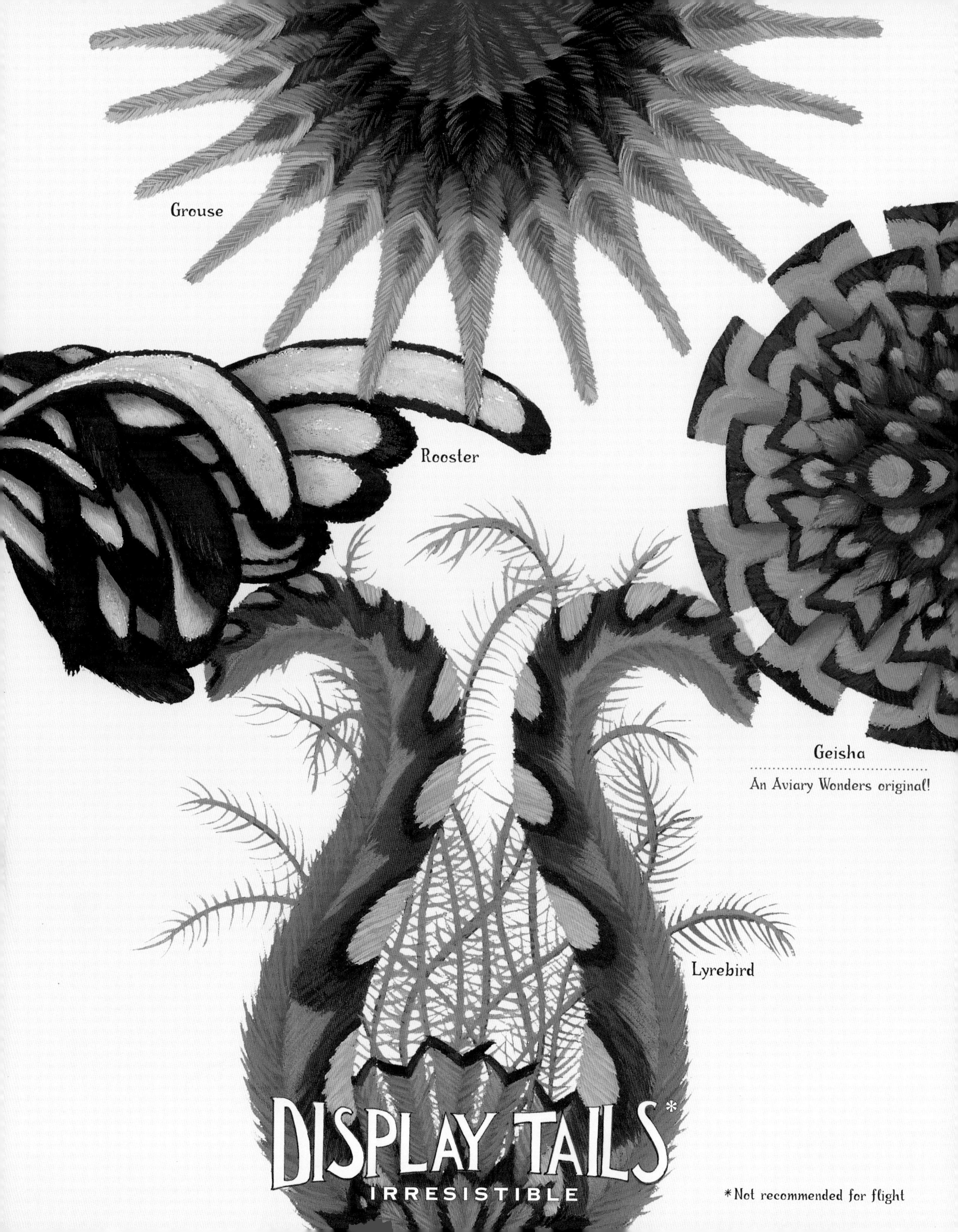

Grouse

Rooster

Geisha

An Aviary Wonders original!

Lyrebird

DISPLAY TAILS*

IRRESISTIBLE

*Not recommended for flight

LEGS and FEET

Will your bird be strolling the beach, lounging in a tree, or stalking its next meal? Select legs and feet that reflect habitat and lifestyle.

FLIGHTLESS

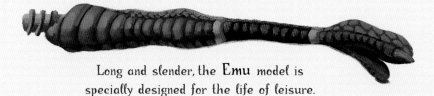

Long and slender, the Emu model is specially designed for the life of leisure.

birds of prey

Owl

Caracara

Adios, Guadalupe Caracara
(early 1900s)

Eagle

R.I.P., Haast's Eagle
(1400s)

PERCHERS

Automatic locking device allows your bird to cling to a branch and sleep in a tree, just like in nature!

Nuthatch

Woodpecker

Passenger Pigeon

Imagine! These birds once traveled in flocks a mile wide and 300 miles long! The last died in 1914.

Swimmers & Waders

Cormorant

Grebe

Gallinule

Coot

LEGS DOs AND DON'Ts

Your bird's proportions must be balanced.

FLIGHT

WING SHAPE AFFECTS FLYING STYLE.
CHOOSE WINGS ACCORDINGLY.
(SEE PAGES 16–17.)

Heron travels with enviable grace
and ease in slow, flapping flight.

Fancy a bird that's quick
and agile and can move
up, down, and sideways
as easily as a helicopter?
Choose Hummingbird.

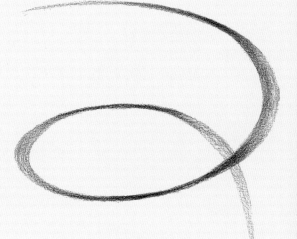

Finch flight is bouncing and elusive.
Compact, rounded wings allow for artful
dodging, fast takeoffs, and efficient
short-distance flying. Ideal
for small birds.

Care to impress, astonish, or even
frighten your neighbors? Select
Peregrine. The wings contract to
let your bird dive at speeds of
up to 175 miles per hour!

PATTERNS

Gull bespeaks nonchalance. Narrow, tapered wings allow your bird to fly at a comfortable clip, cruise without flapping in an updraft, and cover long distances.

Buzzard gives your bird an air of authority. These powerful wings are designed for making sharp turns and soaring in the thermals.

Only **Pheasant** offers such sleek, straight flight lines. Rapid flapping followed by a long glide suggests confidence and determination.

WINGS

Peregrine

Pheasant

Heron

Finch

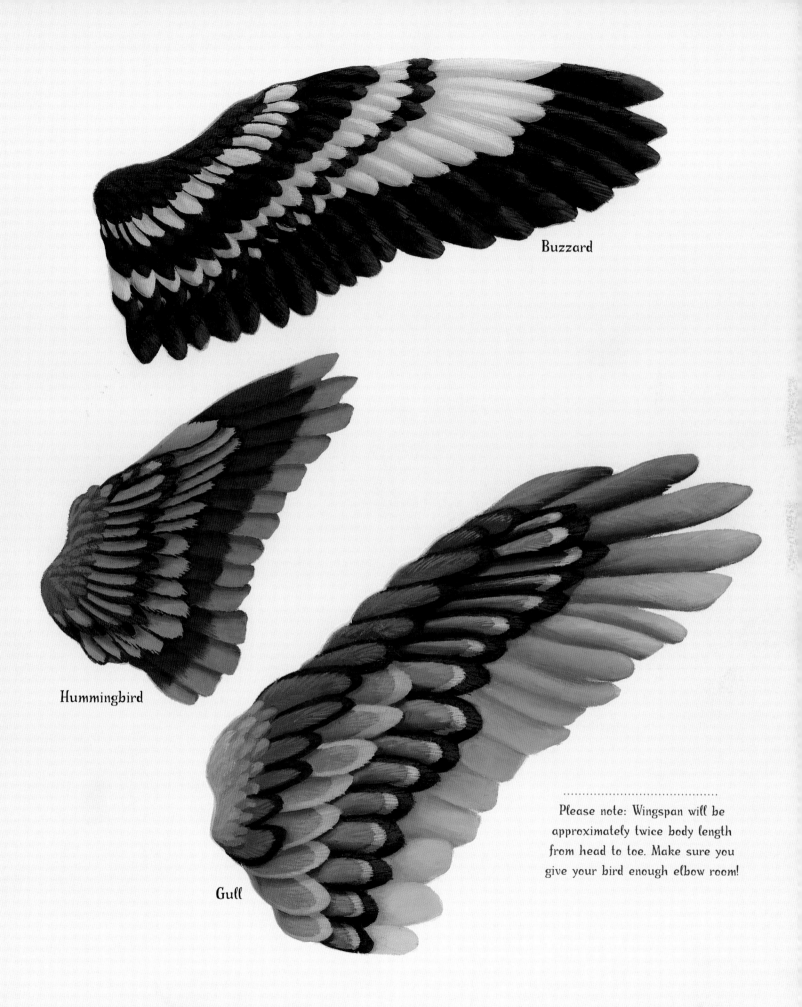

Buzzard

Hummingbird

Gull

Please note: Wingspan will be approximately twice body length from head to toe. Make sure you give your bird enough elbow room!

Style Gallery

Embellishments make your bird unforgettable.

COLLARS

Carnegie

Getty

Rockefeller

Hearst

Biddle

CRESTS

Centurion

Drum Major

Einstein's Brow

Macaroni

Granny Warhol

High~Five

Rabble Rouser

Rockette

Nosegay

Longwave

Isadora Duncan

Beethoven

Samuel Clemens

Aphrodite

Audubon

WATTLE and COMB

Made from recycled rubber for the
look and feel of genuine rooster.
Attractive on any bird.

Rachel Carson

Thoreau

Assembly Instructions

❧ STEP 1 ❧

Making your Bird Feel at Home

- Remove bird immediately from ventilated box and place on pillow.

- Pour one packet of Aviary Wonders Welcome Mix™ into small bowl and stir in ¼ cup warm water.

- Feed bird with free enclosed Aviary Wonders First Day Feeding Spoon™.

- Allow bird to rest for 24 hours in quiet room. Feed one packet of Welcome Mix every 4–6 hours.

STEP 2
ATTACHING THE BEAK

- Fasten straps over head and under chin.
- Adjust for snug but comfortable fit.

A. Snap together.

Attach 24 hours after bird arrives so that it can feed itself.

B. Pull to tighten.

IMPORTANT: Bird must be in a very relaxed state for steps 3, 4, and 5. Feed it a large meal and a glass of warm milk and allow it to fall asleep.

❧ STEP 3 ❧

ATTACHING the TAIL

○ Place tail decorative side down on a table and open cummerbund so it lies flat.

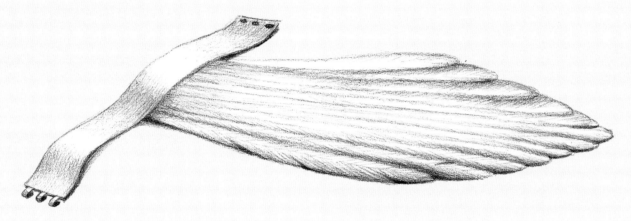

○ Gently set sleeping bird on top of tail and fasten cummerbund around its waist.

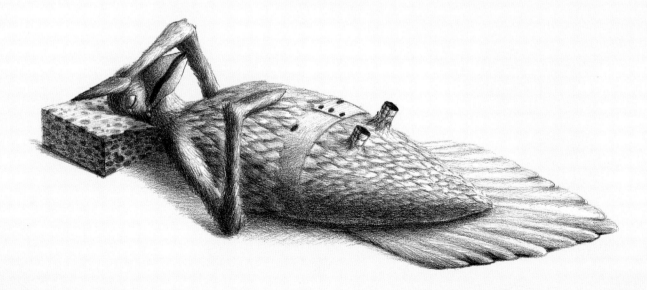

STEP 4
ATTACHING the LEGS

Please note: Feet are marked L and R on the bottom.

- Insert left leg into left opening. Rotate clockwise until securely fastened.

- Repeat process with right leg on right side.

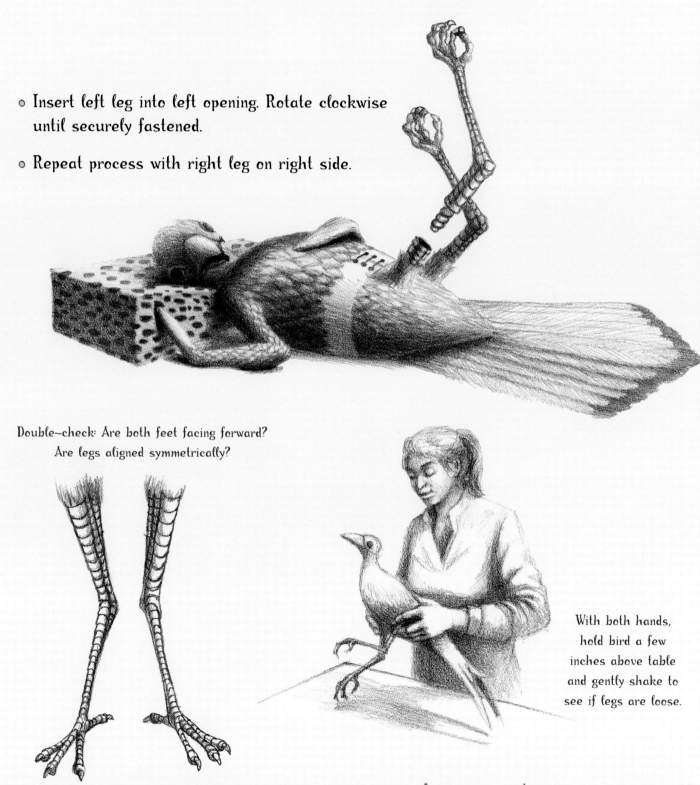

Double~check: Are both feet facing forward? Are legs aligned symmetrically?

With both hands, hold bird a few inches above table and gently shake to see if legs are loose.

❧ STEP 5 ❧
ATTACHING the WINGS

This is a two~person job. To avoid mishaps, read directions carefully before beginning.

Spread wings out on table, decorative side down.

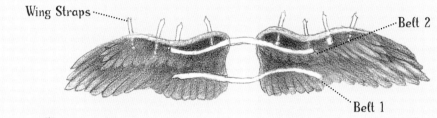

Wing Straps ···········   ··········· Belt 2

··········· Belt 1

PERSON 1: Gently place bird on its back on top of wings. Align shoulders with belts.

PERSON 2: Place one hand on bird's belly to keep it relaxed and still throughout the process. With free hand, extend one of bird's arms into fully outstretched position.

PERSON 1: Fasten each pair of wing straps snugly, beginning with innermost pair.

PERSON 1 & PERSON 2: Repeat procedure with other arm.

PERSON 1: Slip each end of Belt 1 through correct (L or R) slot in the cummerbund. Cross each end of Belt 2 diagonally across chest and fasten buckles.

DRESSING UP
~ OPTIONAL ~

Wattle and Comb
Simply slip over the head like a bathing cap and fasten 3 hooks.

1
2
3

Collar
Snap up the front.

Crest

Hook here

and here.

✤ STEP 6 ✤
TEACHING YOUR BIRD TO FLY

○ First teach your bird to land. Stack three or four books on the ground and set your bird on top.

○ Tempt your bird to hop down by placing a small snack on the ground in front of it. Gradually increase the number of books in the stack until the bird can land without tumbling.

○ Cup both hands under your bird's belly and raise it over your head. Give it a moment to overcome any fear of heights and begin to flap its wings. Pay close attention! When you feel the bird starting to lift, let go!

The first several flights may be short and clumsy. Do not be critical! Flight will improve with practice.

Double-check: All parts must be securely attached before your bird learns to fly.

STEP 7

TEACHING YOUR BIRD TO SING

This takes time, effort, and persistence!

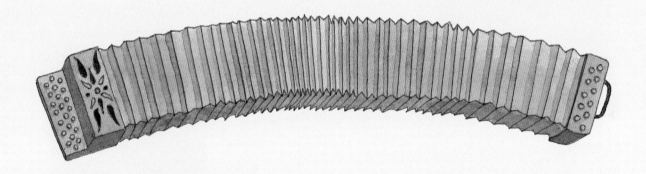

- Select the instrument that you want your bird to imitate. Choose carefully! For example, don't choose the concertina unless you *really* love the concertina!

- Start with a short, simple tune. Sing it or play it on your instrument and allow the bird to copy it. Repeat as necessary. Be patient! Build repertoire slowly. For best results, practice several hours per day.

Troubleshooting

Please send photo with question.

Q. My bird eats all day long! It doesn't do *anything else!* I had hoped it would solve our mouse problem, but all it eats is nuts. What can I do?

A. You've put a nut eater's beak on a bird of prey's body. Luckily, there's an easy solution. Just order a new beak.

Q. We have a beautiful bird, but my son taught it to sing "Old MacDonald Had a Farm." If I hear that song one more time, I may lose my mind. I have tried earplugs and meditation, and I simply cannot bear it anymore. What can I do?

A. It may be time to share your bird with the rest of the world. A pair of Gull wings will allow it to soar across the ocean and discover new things . . . maybe even people who have never heard the song before!

Q. My bird spends a lot of time with its head down. Is it depressed?

A. Possibly, but probably not. It looks top-heavy. Try removing the wattle and comb or using a smaller beak and see if it perks up.

Q. My bird walks in circles until it gets dizzy and falls over. What explains this strange habit?

A. You may have attached the legs incorrectly. Make sure they are fastened tightly and symmetrically.

Q. My bird flies very low to the ground. I've tried wings in every size. What else can I do?

A. It sounds as if your bird is afraid of heights. Try using some encouraging words.

Q. I ordered a bird of prey, but I didn't expect it to look so frightening. It's scaring my children. What can I do?

A. Adding the right crest or collar will soften your bird's appearance. For example, it's bound to look less intimidating wearing the Granny Warhol in pink.

Q. My bird disappears for days at a time. Whenever it does, I worry myself sick. Do you sell birdcages?

A. Absolutely not! Flight is what makes a bird a bird—unless it's a flightless bird, of course. You could replace your bird's tail with a display model. Your bird will still be able to fly, but not as far (or as gracefully).

AVIARY WONDERS INC.

ORDER FORM

1. Choose body size (length from end to end).

2. To build a traditional bird, select all parts from the same category (i.e., Waders or Birds of Prey). To build an entirely new bird of your invention, mix and match parts.

3. Pick your palette. Choose one for the whole bird, or a different one for each part.

Part	Size	Style Name	Color Palette
Body	2 ft. 0 in.	KITE	OLD MASTER
Beak		LAUGHING OWL	"
Tail		WIGEON	TONALIST
Legs		CARACARA	OLD MASTER
Wings		PEREGRINE	"
Collar		HEARST	TONALIST
Crest		RABBLE ROUSER	OLD MASTER
Wattle & Comb		NONE	NONE

Palette options: Old Master, Impressionist, Tonalist, Minimalist

All parts are made to order. Allow 12–16 weeks for delivery.

Disclaimers: Aviary Wonders Inc. offers alternatives to natural birds, not replacements for them. Our birds are guaranteed to fly (we cannot promise graceful flight) and to sing (we are not responsible for quality, texture, or tone of voice). They do not lay eggs or otherwise reproduce. The personality, habits, and manners of each bird are individual and influenced by the owner; they are not the responsibility of the company. Diet is determined by beak shape; appetite is not. Some birds eat more than others; be prepared. Freedom is essential to your bird. Do not keep it in a cage.

JEFFERSON COUNTY LIBRARY
620 Cedar Avenue
Port Hadlock, WA 98339
(360) 385-6544 www.jclibrary.info